A BAND OF BABIES

Written by
Carole Gerber

Illustrated by
Jane Dyer

HARPER
An Imprint of HarperCollinsPublishers

Library of Congress Control Number: 2016942117

ISBN 978-0-06-168955-0

The artist used an assortment of colored pencils (including Prismacolor Premier, Caran d'Ache Prismalo I
and II, Bruynzeel Design, and Derwent) on Canson Mi-Tientes paper to create the illustrations for this book.

Typography by Rachel Zegar

17 18 19 20 21 SCP 10 9 8 7 6 5 4 3 2 1

First Edition

To my bright and mischievous son-in-law, Ben Abzug
—C.G.

To David and Davin, and their babies
—J.D.

Play-group morning. Babies fret—
not sure what to do just yet.

In struts Benny—new in town.
Babies' frowns turn upside down.

"Hi!" says Benny, waves his cup.
Babies happy. Something's up!

Baby Benny spies a box.
Pulls out toys.
Play group rocks!

"Sticks!" says Benny.
Babies cheer.
"Go!" says Benny. "Out of here."

Baby Benny leads the way.
Babies shimmy.
Babies sway.

Beat on drums.
Hooray! Hooray!

Babies hungry, want to eat.
"Walk!" says Benny.
"Find a treat."

"There!" says Benny.
"Walk some more."
Wiggle, giggle to the store.

Thump-a-thump.
Toot! Toot! Whee!
Babies on a shopping spree.

Babies walk inside and smile.

Follow Benny down an aisle.

He grabs a cart.

Three walk beside.

Two climb into the cart and ride.

Four grab cartons.
Two clutch cans.
Quiet babies; busy hands!

Bottles bounce.
Boxes tumble.
Toilet paper in a jumble!

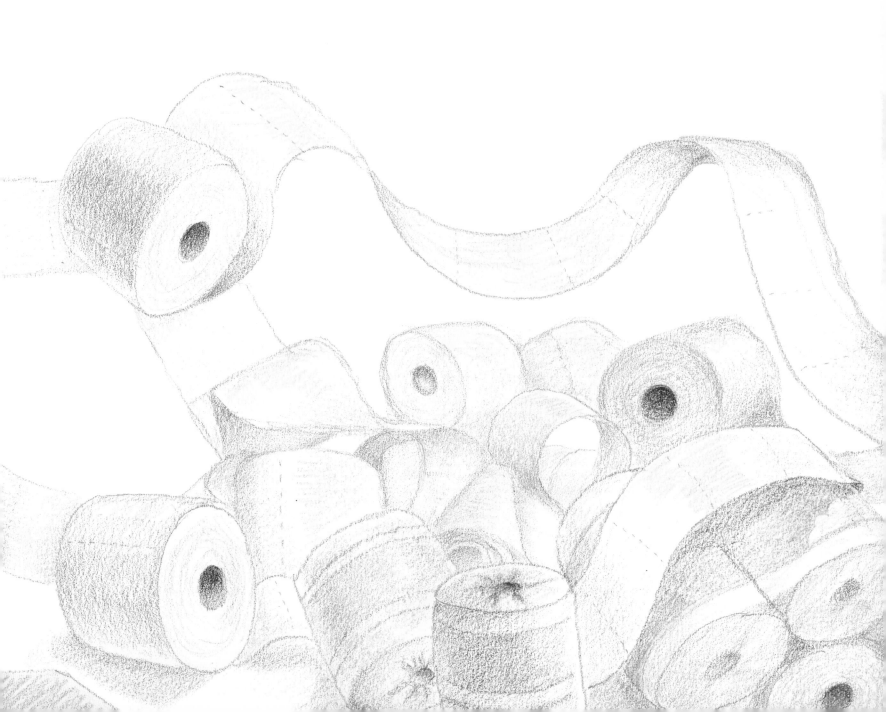

Thump-a-thump.
Toot! Toot! Whee!

Time for snacks.
Yippee! Yippee!

Grapes. Bananas. Apricots.
Hungry babies eating lots.

Carrots. Yogurt.
Love this store!

Benny bellows, "Eat some more!"

Crackers. Pretzels. Bagel chips.
Crumbs coat every baby's lips.

Babies thirsty.
Gulp down juice.
Getting tired of running loose.

Babies wobble.

Babies stoop.

Babies' eyelids start to droop.

Babies drop their drums and flute.

No *thump-a-thump.*
No more *toot, toot.*

Babies fall into a heap.
Shhh!

Even Benny is asleep.